Poka and Peanut Playtime Poems

ISBN: 979-8-218-26775-9

Visit us at PokaSpeaks.com

WRITTEN BY ALEXANDRIA COX
ILLUSTRATED BY ROBERT SEGURA

WHO ARE YOU?

When I get all grown up,
you'll be proud!

Just support me
and help me out!

I'm a little black boy
strong and proud!

Here is my homeland,
here is my crown.

I'm a little black girl
strong and proud!

Here is my homeland,
here is my crown.

When I get all grown up,
you'll be proud!

Just support me
and help me out!

LOOK AT ME

Mama, mama
look at me!
I'm something for the world to see!

My friends may doubt me... but I believe,
I can be whatever I want to be!

Daddy, daddy
look at me!
I'm something for the
world to see!
My friends may doubt me... but I believe,
I can be whatever I want to be!

MiRROR

When I look in the mirror,
do you know what I see?
I see a young black king
looking back at me!

Although, times get tough...
I know one thing!
The only thing better than me,
is a better me.

When I look in the mirror,
do you know what I see?
I see a young black Queen
looking back at me!

Although, times get tough...
I know one thing!
The only thing better than me,
is a better me.

RESPONSIBILITIES

In a world full of responsibilities, what should I be?

An

ctress, an astronaut, or an attorney?

Maybe I should be a

aller

or a

EO.

I don't know, but God will show me the way to go.

In a world full of responsibilities what should I be?

A

D entist, a developer, or a dancer?

or maybe an

E conomist or an EMT.

I'm not sure but God will show me what's for me.
In a world full of responsibilities, I just want to be… A wonderful addition to society.

P-E-T-T-Y

If they be mean to you,
don’t be mean back.
That's P-E-T-T-Y!

Don’t be petty
just say bye-bye.

You can't be number one
if you keep acting like number two.
Lead by example,
show them how bosses move!

Hopefully one day
they'll be a boss like you!

LIFE

Life goes up and life goes down.
Twist, bumps, and turn-arounds.
It's kind of like flying a kite.
You have to do a little running
before things catch flight.

Life goes up and life goes down.
Twist, bumps, and turn-arounds.
It's kind of like drawing a crown.
Your pencil goes many different ways,
but somehow it ends up round.

BIG HEART

There once was a girl with such a BIG HEART, she didn't know what to do. She would help everyone, including me and you. Until one day she needed help and didn't know what to do.

Her grandpa explained that helping people is okay, but you have to make sure that you have someone there when it's time for you.

There once was a boy with such a BIG HEART, he didn't know what to do.

He would help everyone, including me and you. Until one day he needed help and didn't know what to do.

His grandma explained that helping people is okay but you have to make sure that you have someone there when it's time for you.

It's one thing that their grandparents did not know that they knew...

Helping others only makes God want to help you.

BUSINESS

I'm a **CEO**,
you have an **LLC**
and they have a **501C3**.
The world has roles that have to be played.
The best thing about it is...

WE ALL GET PAID!

Business is business but we must see...
that the business world has
NO LIMIT economically.

CEO - Chief executive officer
LLC - limited liability company
501C3 - organization number to indicate they are a nonprofit group with a dedicated mission

CHOICES

Our lives are the products of our choices.
What will you pick?

The **Misfit?**

Healthy and **Fit?**

Or Beautiful and Thick?
You may not know now
but whatever you pick,
remember it's your life
and it's about what you see fit.

Oh Daddy, I want to be like you.
BIG AND STRONG,
and know what to do!

Oh mama, I want to be like you.
It's like you got 8 ARMS
you are always doing the do!

Oh Granny, I want to be like you.

You COOK WITHOUT MEASURING,
it's like the food tells you!

Oh Pawpaw, I want to be just like you.

You are ALWAYS TALKING,
but your lips never move!

Oh baby, we want to be just like you.

A WALKING SPONGE,
you know what everybody do!

YOU ARE WHAT YOU EAT!

Daddy said...

"You are what you eat"
so I pick beans
to replace my meat.

Mama said...

"You are what you eat"
so I pick healthy things like
baby bananas
as my sweet.

Granny said...
"you are what you drink"
so I pick **spring water**
instead of sweet tea.
Pawpaw said...
"you are what you think"
so I pick **success**
when I think of me.

LA-LA-LU

Memaw's famous La-La-Lu.
Also known as survival stew.
Vegetables, Beans, Pasta, and Rice,
all drenched in tomato sauce and served real nice.
We never knew the ingredients,
we just knew that she did the do.
A bowl full of wonders and love
La-La-Lu.
Memaw's Survival Stew,
if the dogs don't like it,
I do!

TEXAS

I live in Texas!
where it's cold and rainy one day,
then it's hot and sunny the next!

And if you wait five minutes
you just might see
some sleet
or snow,
but *youuuu* should know
that sleet and snow
don't stick!
But living in Texas

WILL MAKE YOU SICK!!!

THINGS TO REMEMBER

I SHOULD listen more than I speak.

I SHOULD walk the way that I talk.

I SHOULD stand for what I believe.

I SHOULD have faith in what I want to achieve.

I SHOULD be what the world needs.

I SHOULD BE A BETTER ME.

CLEAN

Wash your hands,
brush your teeth,

clean your face,
and take a bath

To dry off,
we stomp our feet
and to stay clean,
WE REPEAT!

www.ingramcontent.com/pod-product-compliance
Lightning Source LLC
Chambersburg PA
CBHW081127300726
48982CB00005B/871

* 9 7 9 8 2 1 8 2 6 7 7 5 9 *